BIG BLUE SKY
MAKES A
RAINBOW

Written by G.C. Wells

Hello Orange, as **Red** waves to Orange.

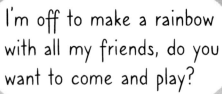

I'm off to make a rainbow with all my friends, do you want to come and play?

Hello Yellow, as **Red** and **Orange** wave to Yellow.

We're off to make a rainbow with all our friends, do you want to come and play?

Hello Green, as **Red**, Orange and Yellow wave to Green.

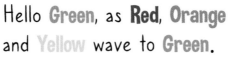

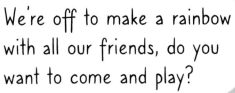
We're off to make a rainbow with all our friends, do you want to come and play?

Thank you to Marlene.

Printed in Great Britain
by Amazon